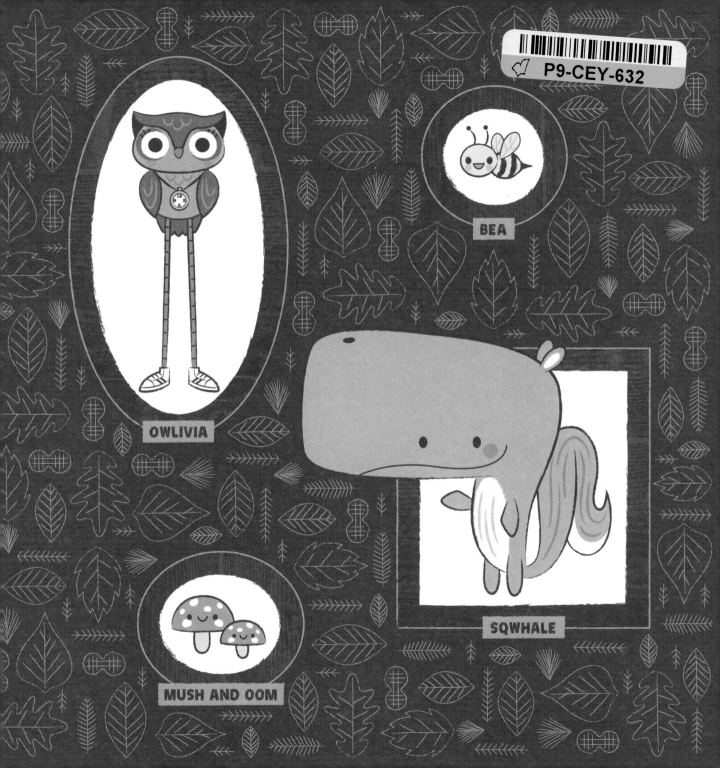

OWLIVIA

BEA

MUSH AND OOM

SQWHALE

For Russell, Marc, and Curtis

Peanut Bear
SEEDS of FRIENDSHIP

WRITTEN AND ILLUSTRATED BY

RALPH COSENTINO

In the magical forest of Yippity Yay,
Peanut Bear played hide-and-go-seek with his friends.

Cowbunny Bo liked to hide with Unicorny
because he told jokes. Owlivia and Bea enjoyed
hiding behind birch trees. Sqwhale, Mush,
and Oom liked cozy hollow logs.

They were all the best of friends.

OH NO!

One day while they were playing,
Bea accidentally buzzed into a branch.
She fell into the stream!

Peanut Bear jumped in to help her,
but the stream carried them both away.

Luckily, Cowbunny Bo had a rope under his hat!
Everyone worked together to pull Peanut
Bear and Bea out of the water.

Poor little Bea's wing was hurt.

You are
so wise,
Owlivia!

Peanut Bear wanted to do something special
for Bea while it healed. "Let's grow her favorite
flower, the Chocolate Cosmos!" said Owlivia.
"We can get seeds from Farmer Fox!"

They began their journey to the other side of the forest.
The path to Farmer Fox's house went through Rainbow Falls,
and they couldn't get across the water. Then Nessie popped up.

She helped Peanut Bear and his friends to the other side and back on the path. "Hip hip hooray!" cheered Peanut Bear. "Our new friend, Nessie, helped us on our way!"

Next they had to pass through Skull Canyon.
Someone big and mean-looking was blocking their way!
It was Minotaur Mike.

"To pass through Skull Canyon, you must first face four challenges!" Mike said.

After finishing the challenges and making friends,
Minotaur Mike let Peanut Bear and his pals pass.

They followed the trail through Skull Canyon.
As they walked around a bend, they found
a giant boulder blocking the path!

Suddenly, it was lifted.
"I thought my new friends might need some help!"
Mike said. "Hip hip hooray!" cheered Sqwhale.
"Mike helped us on our way!"

Thanks to their new friend, they reached the farm at the end of the path. Farmer Fox was happy to help and gave Peanut Bear a basket of Chocolate Cosmos seeds.

Peanut Bear and his friends went straight home and began planting the seeds. It was very hard work.

As soon as they planted a seed in the soil, a snird swooped down and gobbled it up! Peanut Bear and his friends tried chasing them away, but they kept coming back.

Unicorny became angrier and angrier until . . .

The snirds left the seeds
and ate the popcorn instead!

They gave the garden lots of sun and water.
The seeds quickly grew and grew.

One morning, Bea smelled the scent of something really good.

The Chocolate Cosmos had blossomed!
"Thanks for being such great friends," Bea said.

One Mississippi,
two Mississippi . . .

With the sweet scent of flowers in the air,
Peanut Bear and his pals cheered, "Hip hip hooray!"
They were looking forward to new adventures in
the magical forest of Yippity Yay.

The end.

INSIGHT KIDS

An Imprint of Insight Editions
PO Box 3088
San Rafael, CA 94912
www.insighteditions.com

Find us on Facebook: www.facebook.com/InsightEditions

Follow us on Twitter: @insighteditions

Art and Peanut Bear © 2018 of Ralph Cosentino. All rights reserved.
www.mypeanutbear.com

Library of Congress Cataloging-in-Publication Data available.

ISBN: 978-1-68383-234-8

Publisher: Raoul Goff
Associate Publisher: Elaine Piechowski
Art Director: Chrissy Kwasnik
Designers: Ralph Cosentino and Lauren Chang
Editor: Rebekah Piatte
Editorial Assistant: Kaia Waller
Production Editor: Lauren LePera
Associate Production Manager: Sam Taylor

ROOTS of PEACE   REPLANTED PAPER

Insight Editions, in association with Roots of Peace, will plant two trees for each
tree used in the manufacturing of this book. Roots of Peace is an internationally
renowned humanitarian organization dedicated to eradicating land mines worldwide
and converting war-torn lands into productive farms and wildlife habitats. Roots of
Peace will plant two million fruit and nut trees in Afghanistan and provide farmers
there with the skills and support necessary for sustainable land use.

Manufactured in China by Insight Editions

10 9 8 7 6 5 4 3 2 1

PEANUT BEAR

COWBUNNY BO

UNICORNY